My First Red Panda Book

JENNY KELLETT

BELLANOVA
MELBOURNE · SOFIA · BERLIN

My name is...

Hey there! I'm Rosy the red panda.

Red pandas are cute animals that live in the forests.
Can you find me in the forest?

Red pandas live in forests on the **mountains** in Asia.
Can you point to the mountain?

Sometimes it snows in the mountains! But red pandas stay warm with their **fluffy fur**.

Help me get home!
Draw a line on the map to where you think I live.
Hint: look for the mountains and bamboo!

ASIA

Mmm,
yummy!
Red pandas love to
eat bamboo.

Do you know which of these plants is bamboo? Hint: it's tall and green!

Red pandas
have beautiful,
bushy tails!

Can you count the stripes on my tail?
Hint: there's more than 5!

Peek-a-boo!
Can you see
me hiding in
the tree?

Red pandas are great climbers.
Have you ever climbed a tree?

Red pandas love sleeping high up in the trees!
Zzzz...

Red pandas use their tails
as warm, fluffy pillows!

Can you curl up like a
red panda using your
arm as a pillow?

Red pandas eat more than just bamboo. They also love fruits, berries, and acorns!

Let's play a game!
Point to the foods that I like to eat!

Huff-quack!
Squeal!
Twitter!

Let's make some red panda sounds!
Can you squeal, twitter, or huff-quack like a red panda?!

Red pandas prefer to live alone.

Sleeping

Eating

Point to the pictures of what
you like to do too!

Climbing

Playing

Red panda babies are called cubs!
Red panda moms take great care of their kids!

Bears

Tigers

Raccoons

Pandas

Red pandas need our help! Their homes are disappearing.

But you can help
by planting trees
and keeping the
forest clean.

Help the red panda find its way **home**!

Find the path that leads the red panda to a healthy forest.

*Remember: A healthy forest is **clean** and has lots of **bamboo**!*

What is your favorite thing about red pandas?

Can you name two foods red pandas eat?

How can we help keep red pandas safe?

Congratulations!

Name: ....

For learning all about

RED PANDAS

And becoming a Red Panda Expert

Jenny Kellett
Author

ALSO BY JENNY KELLETT

Find us on **YouTube** for weekly animal videos just for kids!

... **and more!**

Available at

www.bellanovabooks.com

and all major online bookstores.

9 782487 191167